ROSE FACES THE MUSIC
by L.E. Williams

Illustrations by
Bill Dodge

Spot Illustrations by
Rich Grote

MAGIC ATTIC PRESS

Published by Magic Attic Press.

This book is dedicated to Madison Rebecca Mullen with love.

For more information contact:
Book Editor, Magic Attic Press, 866 Spring Street,
P.O. Box 9722, Portland, ME 04104-5022

First Edition
Printed in the United States of America
1 2 3 4 5 6 7 8 9 10

Magic Attic Club is a registered trademark.

Betsy Gould, Publisher
Marva Martin, Art Director
Jay Brady, Managing Editor

Edited by Susan Korman
Designed by Cindy Vacek

Library of Congress Cataloging · in · Publication Data
Williams, L.E.
Rose Faces the Music / by L.E. Williams:
illustrations by Bill Dodge, spot illustrations by Rich Grote.--1st ed.
p. cm.-- (Magic Attic Club)
Summary: On another adventure through the mirror in the magic attic, Rose
finds herself chosen to play a saxophone solo in a jazz performance at the
presidential inaugural celebration.
ISBN 1-57513-108-0 (hardback). -- ISBN 1-57513-107-2 (paperback)
(1. Space and time--Fiction. 2. Musicians--Fiction)
I. Dodge, Bill, ill. II. Grote, Rich, ill. III. Title. IV. Series.
PZ7.W666583Ro 1997   (Fic)--dc21   97-27263   CIP AC

Magic Attic Club books are printed on acid-free, recycled paper.

As members of the
MAGIC ATTIC CLUB,
we promise to
be best friends,
share all of our adventures in the attic,
use our imaginations,
have lots of fun together,
and remember—the real magic is in us.

Alison   Keisha

Heather   Megan

Rose

Table of Contents

Prologue

When Alison, Heather, Keisha, and Megan find a gold key buried in the snow, they have no idea that it will change their lives forever. They discover that it belongs to Ellie Goodwin, the owner of an old Victorian house across the street from Alison's. Ellie, grateful when they return the key to her, invites the girls to play in her attic. There they find a steamer trunk filled with wonderful outfits—party dresses, a princess gown, a ballet tutu, cowgirl clothes, and many, many, more. Excited, the girls try on some of the costumes and admire their reflections in a tall gilded mirror nearby. Suddenly they are transported to a new time and place, embarking on the greatest adventure of their lives.

When they return to the present and Ellie's attic, they form the Magic Attic Club, promising to tell each other every exciting detail of their future adventures through the mirror.

Chapter
One

CRASH

And she scores again!" shouted the announcer.

The crowd went wild, cheering and clapping and stomping their feet on the bleachers.

Rose Hopkins stood up behind the desk and bowed to her imaginary fans. She had to do something to keep from falling asleep while she transferred a bunch of files onto a floppy disk for her mother. The job was so boring and was taking so long. On the other hand, pretending she was an Olympic soccer player was a blast—especially since she was scoring points one after another.

As the next file was being copied, Rose stared out the window. Blue and red curtains framed a beautiful day outside. That was where she wanted to be, not cooped up inside doing *uninteresting* stuff on the computer.

The doorbell rang downstairs, and she heard her grandfather answer it. Then footsteps thundered up the steps.

Keisha Vance, Heather Hardin, Megan Ryder, and Alison McCann all burst into the room.

"Don't tell me you're doing your homework," Keisha groaned as they crowded into the small office. "You have all weekend to do that."

Rose grinned. "Actually, I'm doing my *mom's* homework."

"Your mother has homework?" Megan asked, pushing the sleeves up on her sweatshirt.

"She's taking courses in anthropology at the university," Rose explained. "I'm just transferring a bunch of files for her onto one disk. She needs them tomorrow for a project in one of her classes."

Alison frowned. "Does that mean you don't have time for those soccer tips you promised to show us?"

Rose rocked back in her chair. "Oh, I totally forgot about that, Ali."

"You said you'd show us how to improve our kicking technique," Keisha reminded her. "The way you learned it at the soccer clinic you went to last month."

"Right," Alison chimed in eagerly. "I want to improve my skills so I can show off in front of my brothers. They all think they're the greatest soccer players in the world."

Rose couldn't help smiling at the determined look on her friend's face. Alison was a very good athlete, and very competitive when it came to sports. Rose wasn't a natural athlete like Alison, but had worked hard to be good at soccer. She'd been playing the sport for a long time, and she was eager to teach her friends some of the skills that she'd learned.

Rose pushed back a strand of her long, dark hair. I'm sure I could finish the work for my mother later tonight, or tomorrow morning, she thought.

She jumped up. "Let's go!"

"Are you sure?" Megan asked, motioning to the computer. "We don't want to get you in trouble."

Rose headed for the door. "Don't worry, I can finish later." As she ran downstairs, she pulled her thick hair back into a ponytail, using a scrunchie she kept around her wrist. She loved the way her long hair swished against her back when she moved, but when she played soccer, she had to keep it out of her face.

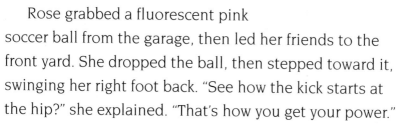

Rose grabbed a fluorescent pink soccer ball from the garage, then led her friends to the front yard. She dropped the ball, then stepped toward it, swinging her right foot back. "See how the kick starts at the hip?" she explained. "That's how you get your power."

As each of her friends tried the kick, aiming at an imaginary ball, Rose gave them pointers. "I think you need to turn your foot out, Heather, just like in ballet...More from the hip, Keisha...Ali, that looks great."

"Now let's practice on a real ball," Rose suggested. "You can go first, Megan."

Megan took a few running steps toward the ball and smacked it with her foot. The ball veered off into the bushes. "Oops," she murmured, her face turning red with embarrassment.

"That's okay, Megan," Rose said as she scrambled to retrieve the ball. "You just have to aim next time. Lesson number two is to look at the point where you want the ball to go."

"Just like in tennis, Megan," Alison chimed in. "Let me try."

Rose tossed her the ball.

Alison rushed forward at full speed and kicked. She missed the ball completely.

The other girls stood in stunned silence. Rose couldn't believe it. Alison—the best athlete of the bunch—had actually missed!

Alison dropped to the grass and started howling with laughter. "I totally blew it!" she exclaimed. "Just don't tell my brothers!"

"At least I connected with the ball," Megan teased her.

"Lesson number three," Alison said through her laughter. "Don't miss the ball!"

Heather helped Alison to her feet, then she turned to Rose. "Maybe you'd better give us a full demonstration before it's my turn."

"Okay," Rose said. "You guys go over there and block my kick." She waved toward the front part of her lawn, just beyond the flower beds.

She picked up the ball and hit it in the air with her right knee. She kept the ball bouncing in the air as she tapped it with alternating knees and the inside part of her ankles. Her friends cheered.

"You're awesome," Keisha said. "How do you do that?"

Rose didn't take her eyes off the ball. "Practice," she explained.

Finally Rose let the ball drop to the grass. She pulled her leg back and aimed, leading with her hip. A second later, the fluorescent pink sphere soared into the air.

Heather, Alison, Keisha, and Megan all jumped for it, but it whizzed over their fingertips.

Rose's eyes widened with horror as the ball continued its flight, right across the street and into the open window of a parked car. The ball landed with a sickening crash.

Chapter
Two

LESSON NUMBER FOUR

Rose winced and closed her eyes. For a moment, no one said anything. All five girls just stared at the open window.

"That sounded like breaking glass," Alison said.

"We'd better go see," Heather said, heading across the street.

Rose jogged to catch up to her friends as they reached the

car. As she peered through the window, her stomach sank. A lamp lay in shattered pieces all over the passenger's side. Her ball sat quietly in the middle of the wreckage.

"I'm sorry we couldn't stop the ball," Heather said, placing a hand on Rose's shoulder. "I guess we wouldn't make very good goalies."

"Whose car is this anyway?" Keisha asked. She walked around to the back. It had an out-of-state license plate.

Rose shrugged. "I've never seen it on this street before."

"We'd better leave a note for the owner," Keisha continued. "You know, so we can offer to pay for the lamp."

"There goes all my savings," Alison muttered. "I'll bet that lamp was expensive. It looks like an antique."

Rose's knees wobbled. An *antique*? She reached in the window and grabbed her ball, tucking it under her arm.

"And it wasn't even our fault," Megan added.

Rose opened her mouth, about to take all the blame.

"I mean," Megan added hurriedly, glancing at Rose, "it was just an accident."

Rose shut her mouth. Megan was right—it was just an accident after all.

"I have a piece of paper and a pen here," Megan said,

digging a small notepad out of the back pocket of her jeans. "I carry them around in case I get a good story idea I don't want to forget." She pulled a pen out of her other pocket and began writing.

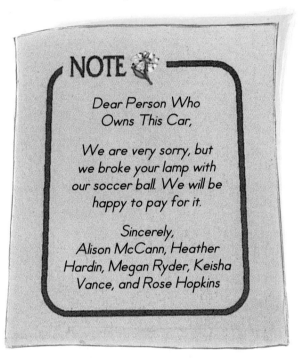

NOTE

Dear Person Who Owns This Car,

We are very sorry, but we broke your lamp with our soccer ball. We will be happy to pay for it.

*Sincerely,
Alison McCann, Heather Hardin, Megan Ryder, Keisha Vance, and Rose Hopkins*

"That sounds good," Rose murmured.

Megan slipped the note under the windshield wiper. "I guess I'll go home and tell my mom what happened in case someone calls."

"Me, too," Keisha said.

"See you guys tomorrow," Rose said. As her friends

began to drift away, she noticed that the sky had
darkened and the autumn air was cooler. She glanced at
her watch and groaned. Her mother would be home any
second and she still hadn't finished copying the files for
her. Now she had more bad news about the lamp.

Along the street, lights began to blink on inside the
houses. Rose noticed the soft glow of Ellie Goodwin's
porch light. Suddenly, she had an idea.

"Grandfather," she called inside when she reached the
front porch. "I'm going to Ellie's house for a little while."

"Okay," her grandfather called back from the kitchen.

Rose and her grandfather were very close. They spent every afternoon together getting dinner ready before Rose's parents got home from the university. He often told Rose stories about their Cheyenne heritage, and Rose was teaching him how to use the computer.

Her grandfather apeared on the porch and looked closely at Rose. "Is something bothering you, Little Flower?"

Rose bowed her head. Her grandfather had a way of seeing inside her. Sometimes that was fine, but sometimes it was embarrassing.

He put a hand on her shoulder. "Tell me what's in your heart."

Rose pulled away. She wasn't ready to talk to him—or anyone—about the mistakes she'd made that afternoon. "Nothing's bothering me," she said quickly. "I—I just want to go to Ellie's for a bit."

Before her grandfather could ask any more questions, Rose whirled around and ran all the way to Ellie's house.

Chapter
Three

JAZZ WITH PIZZAZZ

Ellie Goodwin answered the door after the first ring. "Come in, Rose," she said.

"Hi, Ellie." Rose glanced around as she always did, admiring the spacious old house. She loved the dark wood-paneled doors and the high ceilings.

"I'm just tying up some of the herbs I grew in my garden this summer," Ellie said, showing Rose a bundle of green

stalks. "I'll hang them upside down in the pantry until they're dry. Then I can use snippets of them all winter." She held the bundle under Rose's nose. "Smell that."

Rose took a deep breath. "Mmmm, lavender," she said, instantly recognizing the sweet odor.

Ellie looked surprised.

"My grandfather taught me a lot about herbs," Rose explained proudly. "He has an herb garden too."

Ellie peered at Rose. "How are you?" she asked warmly.

Rose shrugged, suddenly feeling shy.

"Would you like to spend some time in the attic?" Ellie asked. "It's a wonderful place to sort through anything that might be troubling you."

"You don't mind?" Rose asked eagerly.

Ellie shook her head. "Not at all. Now shoo," she said kindly, waving Rose away with a bunch of lavender.

Rose gave Ellie a grateful smile before she hurried into the entryway. There she lifted the lid of the silver box on the table and carefully took out the gold key that would unlock the door to the attic.

It didn't take Rose long to reach the top of the attic stairs. Only the dim evening light coming through the windows lit the room. She pulled a silk tasseled cord, and immediately light from the hanging lamp cast a soft glow on everything.

Excitement tingled down Rose's arms. She had been in the attic only a few times, but each time something wonderful had happened. After she'd put on a costume from Ellie's old steamer trunk and looked into the gilded mirror, she was transported to a new time and place.

Eagerly Rose lifted the trunk's heavy lid. Her fingers brushed against a gold ski parka with black trim. Underneath, she spotted a gown made of a shimmering mint-green fabric. Her eyes lingered on it for a moment. The gown had a V neck, short sleeves, and five sparkling stones on the sash. It looked to Rose like a dress that someone might wear to a ball.

As she stood up to try on the beautiful gown, Rose's eyes caught a flash of gold in the trunk: a shiny saxophone lay underneath the dress.

Rose quickly kicked off her sneakers and pulled on the dress. Then she reached for the instrument. A white satin ribbon trimmed in gold hung from the sax. Rose carefully slipped the neck strap over her head, then hurried over to the mirror.

Smiling, Rose lifted the instrument and pretended to play. Her grandfather listened to jazz all the time, and Rose

had always loved the sax's deep, mellow sound. As her fingers ran up and down the keys, she twirled around, letting the wide skirt float out around her.

"You look awesome, Rose," a girl said breathlessly. "The dress looks like it was made for you."

Rose closed her eyes, trying to catch her balance. When she opened them again, she saw that she was standing in a bedroom. A girl about Rose's age, with curly red hair, was staring at her.

"We're going to look so great in our outfits for the concert," the girl went on.

"Oh…I know," Rose stammered. As she looked down, she realized the saxophone was still hanging from her neck.

The red-headed girl reached forward. "Here, give me that. I'll put it in your case for you." She took the instrument out of Rose's hands. "Too bad Casey can't go with us because of her tonsillitis, but our band director, Miss Lum, says you're the perfect person to take her place on the sax."

Rose forced a smile, trying to act as if she knew exactly what the girl was talking about.

Just then a woman called up from downstairs.

"Lizzie! Rose! Are you two almost ready? It's time to take you to the bus."

"We'll be down in a sec, Mom," Lizzie shouted back. Then she turned to Rose. "Here, change into this."

Rose looked at what Lizzie had handed her. It was a blue warm-up suit with the words "Jazz with Pizzazz" embroidered on the back of the jacket in silver thread. On the front, Rose's name was stitched over the heart.

She changed quickly, placing her dress on a pink and white checked padded hanger and slipping it inside a matching travel case. On the outside of the travel case were Rose's initials and inside there were several pairs of neatly folded jeans and T-shirts, as well as an alarm clock, a journal, a small pillow, and a pair of tortoise-shell glasses inside their own small green satin case. Rose took the travel case and followed Lizzie downstairs.

Then, Lizzie's parents loaded the two of them into a minivan and drove to an elementary school about a mile away.

Rose stared at all the people milling around in the parking lot. Floodlights illuminated the area so it almost looked like a movie set. At the far side of the lot, a large bus sat with its motor idling. In front of the bus, a crowd held a banner that read "Good Luck, Jazz with Pizzazz!" in bright neon colors. Obviously all this had something to

do with the jazz
band—but what?
Rose couldn't ask
too many questions
or Lizzie would get

suspicious, but she sure wished she knew what all the
excitement was about.

As Rose and Lizzie jumped out of the van, a short
woman with dark hair and half-glasses hurried over.
"You're here at last, " she exclaimed. "I was about to send
out a search party."

"Rose was just trying on the concert dress, Miss Lum,"
Lizzie explained. "It fits great."

Miss Lum nodded briskly. "Wonderful. Now get on the
bus, and whatever you do, don't forget your instruments!
Or your glasses, Rose," she reminded her. "You need
them for reading the sheet music."

"Good luck!" someone said, patting Rose on the
shoulder.

"Break a leg."

"Make us proud!"

Rose just smiled and nodded the whole time, still
feeling totally clueless. Just as they were about to step
onto the bus, a man's voice came over a loudspeaker.

"Oh, brother," Lizzie said with a moan. "I hope

Principal Davies can keep this speech short, or we'll never get to Washington."

"Ladies and gentlemen, proud parents and students," the principal began. "We're here to wish Jazz with Pizzazz the best of luck. They would like to thank all of you for your support in raising the funds needed for this once-in-a-lifetime opportunity. Have a safe trip, and don't forget to tell the president we wish him well. "

President? Rose thought as everyone cheered. But before she could ask Lizzie exactly what the principal meant, Lizzie motioned for Rose to follow her up the high steps onto the bus.

"Isn't this cool?" Lizzie exclaimed as the bus pulled out of the parking lot.

Rose nodded. "But I…uh…have just one question— what president was the principal talking about?"

Lizzie burst into laughter. "Very funny, Rose," she said. "As if you don't know we're on our way to Washington, D.C., to play at the president's inaugural ball!"

Chapter
Four

A CHANGE IN PLANS

R ose tried not to let her mouth hang open like a gasping fish, but she couldn't help it. She was going to play in a jazz band for the president of the United States? She took a deep breath and leaned her head back against the cushioned headrest. This is so cool, she thought. Then something occurred to her—she didn't know the first thing about playing the saxophone. What was she going to do?

The bus driver announced they'd be driving all night

to get to Washington by dawn. Rose took out her travel pillow and borrowed a blanket from one of the chaperones, but she wasn't sure she'd be able to fall asleep. She had only recently discovered the secret of Ellie's attic, but her friends had told her that the mirror sometimes gave them special talents while they were on adventures. She certainly hoped that was true now.

The early-morning sun coming through the tinted windows of the bus woke Rose.

"Good morning, sleepyhead," Lizzie said. She was sprawled out on the seats on the opposite side of the aisle.

Rose smiled and yawned. "Are we almost there?"

Lizzie grinned. "Look out the window."

Rose did. "Hey, isn't that the—"

Just then the bus microphone clicked on. "Who can tell me who lives at sixteen hundred Pennsylvania Avenue?" asked the bus driver.

"The president!" Rose chimed in with the rest of the band members as they drove slowly by the White House. It looked beautiful, surrounded with fresh snow. A large Christmas tree stood in the center of the lawn, twinkling with lights.

It must be early January, Rose thought, craning her

neck to keep the tree in sight as they turned a corner; she remembered presidential inaugurations always took place at the beginning of the year.

A moment later, Mrs. Krampetz, one of the two chaperones, turned around from the seat in front of them. "We'll tour Washington later today. First we're going to—"

"Practice," Miss Lum broke in with a smile.

"Did you practice your solo?" Lizzie asked, looking at Rose.

Rose blinked. "My what?"

"Your solo," Lizzie repeated.

Rose swallowed hard. "Oh, right, my solo," she managed to say. "Sure. I practiced," she added, trying to hide her worry.

A short while later, the driver pulled up in front of a fancy hotel. The band members were shepherded off the bus and shown to their rooms.

Rose and Lizzie shared a small but very pretty room that overlooked a busy street. The furniture was dark walnut, and a plush burgundy carpet covered the floor. The walls were painted a soft shade of pink.

Before Rose had time to unpack, there was a knock on the door. "Ready?" Miss Lum called. "The bus is waiting to take us to rehearsal."

Rose grabbed her glasses and her instrument case and followed Lizzie to the elevator.

The bus drove them to another hotel, where a clerk led them to a huge ballroom bustling with people decorating and arranging tables and chairs. In the middle was a large stage, set up with chairs, music stands, and microphones.

A few people stood around with cameras, and others were scribbling in small notebooks. When the band entered, everyone turned to look at them.

"Okay, guys, let's go," Miss Lum said, pointing to the stage.

As Rose climbed the stairs to the stage, she saw a group of reporters clustered around Miss Lum, asking questions about their band and their trip to Washington. Seeing some of the photographers taking candid shots,

Rose smoothed her hair, hoping it was still neat. She took a seat between the two other saxophone players. Lizzie was sitting with the other trumpeter. There was also one trombone player, one clarinetist, one percussionist, and one bass player—nine musicians in all.

Rose watched the sax players on either side of her lick their reeds before attaching them to the mouthpieces of their instruments. She copied their motions, and to her relief her hands somehow knew exactly what to do. Feeling more confident, she placed the white, gold-trimmed strap around her neck, opened her music book, and put on the tortoise-shell glasses that she'd found in the suitcase.

The reporters sat down to watch the rehearsal, and Miss Lum shuffled through some music on her own stand. Finally, she raised her hands. "Ready, girls?"

Everyone nodded.

"And a-one, and a-two, and a-one, two, three." On three, Miss Lum's hands started to dance through the air.

Miraculously, Rose was able to follow the beat. Not only that, but her fingers flew over the keys as if she'd been taking lessons for years. A deep, mellow tone wove in and out of the other instruments' sounds.

Hey, this is fun! Rose thought, her foot tapping to the rhythm.

There was only one stressful moment when the music became complicated and Rose's fingers couldn't keep up with the beat.

Miss Lum lowered her hands and shook her head. "No, no, no, saxes. It's *diddi diddi doo dah doo dah dewah*, not *blah blah blah*. Let's try it again."

In fact, they had to try it five more times before Rose's fingers moved as quickly as they were supposed to.

The girl playing the larger sax leaned over. "Don't worry about it, Rose. You're doing great."

Rose smiled gratefully. "I'm just a little nervous about playing in front of the president," she admitted. She noticed the girl's name, Jeanne, embroidered on her jacket.

Jeanne nodded. "We all are. It's so exciting to be here."

Throughout the rehearsal, Rose couldn't help noticing a short man in a gray suit watching them. He wasn't running around getting things ready, and he didn't look like a reporter. He just stood there and stared at them with a frown on his face.

The band finally worked their way through the three pieces they were going to play at the inauguration ball. Miss Lum beamed at them. "Great job, Jazz with Pizzazz!"

The man in the gray suit stepped up to the stage. "This is Jazz with Pizzazz?"

Miss Lum whirled around. "Yes, that's us."

"Where's the rest of the group?" the man demanded.

"What do you mean? " Miss Lum asked, motioning to her musicians. "We're all here."

The man's frown deepened. "You're telling me it's just nine girls?"

Rose could see Miss Lum clench her teeth. "Yes, it's just these *young ladies*. Do you have a problem with that?"

"No, no," the man said quickly. "It's just that when I heard your tape for the contest, I assumed…" He cleared his throat but didn't finish his sentence. Instead, he started to walk away with brisk little steps. "You'll be informed of the final schedule later," he said over his shoulder.

Miss Lum looked flabbergasted. "We already have the final schedule, sir," she called after him. "We're playing at nine o'clock at the main ball." But it was too late. The man had zipped out of the ballroom.

"What did he mean by 'final' schedule?" Lizzie asked.

The director shrugged. "Maybe he doesn't know we already have our schedule. Don't worry, girls," she added soothingly.

But as they packed up their instruments, Rose did worry. She had a terrible feeling that they hadn't heard the last from that man.

When Rose stepped off the stage, a young woman approached her.

"Hi, I'm Sandy Mills from the *Washington Eagle*. Can I ask you a few questions?"

Lizzie nudged Rose in the ribs and grinned.

"Sure," Rose agreed with a smile. A reporter was actually going to interview her for a newspaper article!

The young woman whipped out a notebook and pencil from her bag. After she got basic information such as Rose's name, age, and instrument, she asked, "How do you feel about playing for the president of the United States?"

"I'm thrilled," Rose answered honestly. "But I'm a little nervous, too."

Sandy laughed. "No wonder. It's not every day that your band gets invited to perform at a presidential inauguration." She looked at Rose closely. "So if you could say one thing to the president, Rose, what would it be?"

Rose thought for a moment. "Well, first I'd thank him for the great honor of letting us play at the main inaugural ball," she said carefully. "Then I'd tell him that I hope he works hard on keeping peace around the world during his term."

"Good answer, Rose," the reporter said, nodding and

jotting something down in her notebook. "Thank you for your time. If there's anything that you or Jazz with Pizzazz needs while you're in D.C., give me a call."

This is so cool, Rose thought—playing for the president and being interviewed by a newspaper reporter.

Back at the hotel, as the band members were finishing lunch, a woman wearing a bright red dress walked up.

"I'm Mrs. Pierce," Rose heard her tell Miss Lum. "I'm helping to coordinate the music for the inaugural balls. Here's your revised schedule. Mr. Warton—I believe you met him earlier today—had to make some changes."

Miss Lum looked at the paper. "But it says here we're not playing at the main ball. Why not?"

Mrs. Pierce fiddled with the buttons on her coat. "Mr. Warton felt—well, he had to juggle a few things. I'm very sorry."

Rose's heart sank.

"Will the president hear us?" Lizzie asked.

"Probably not, my dear, " Mrs. Pierce said, looking apologetic. "There are a number of balls all going on at the same time in different places. I'm afraid he can't make it to all of them, even though he'd like to. He has a schedule to keep, too."

The woman bustled away, and the group sat in glum silence. Rose felt sorry for herself, but even sorrier for the rest of Jazz with Pizazz. They had all worked so hard to get there, and now...

"I'm so disappointed," Jeanne murmured. "We practiced our fingers off to make the tape to enter the contest. After we won, I must have baked five hundred dozen chocolate chip cookies to earn the money to get here—all for nothing."

"It's not fair," Lizzie chimed in.

Rose looked at Miss Lum. "Can't we do something?" she asked.

"I'm afraid not," the band director replied with a sigh. "Mr. Warton is the one in charge of tomorrow's schedule. I know it's a big letdown, girls," she went on, "but there's nothing we can do but accept the fact that there's been a change in plans." With that, Miss Lum folded the paper and slipped it into her pocket.

"Come on, girls," one of the chaperones chimed in, trying to sound cheerful. "It's time for our tour of the nation's capital."

Rose followed the rest of the grumbling band out to the bus. She could feel her disappointment turning into anger. She just couldn't accept this sudden change in plans—especially since she had the feeling that Mr. Warton had bumped them on purpose.

I've got to think of something, Rose thought as she took her seat on the bus. But what could she do to get Mr. Warton to change his mind?

Chapter

Five

THE TOUR

O ur first stop on the tour will be the Lincoln
Memorial," the driver called out as the bus pulled
away from the hotel. "Now who can tell me what number
president Mr. Lincoln was?

Rose knew; she just wasn't in the mood to answer.
Neither was anyone else.

The driver glanced at them in the rearview mirror.
"What's wrong with you all? Don't tell me you've never
taken American history," he teased. "Now don't be shy

kids. Who can tell me the answer?"

Finally someone called out, "Lincoln was the sixteenth president."

"Good," the bus driver replied. "One of you did pay attention in class after all. You're absolutely right." As they pulled up to the Lincoln Memorial, he was telling them that there were thirty-six Doric columns in front, one for each state of the Union in the year Lincoln died.

The girls zipped up their coats before leaving the bus.

"It's freezing out," Rose said, hopping up and down to get warmer.

"I know," Lizzie said through chattering teeth. "Let's go look at Lincoln fast so we can get back on the bus and be warm!"

Rose looked up at the mammoth statue of Lincoln. For a moment she forgot the cold biting at her ears and toes. She had seen hundreds of photographs of the monument, but she was thrilled to actually be there in person. She had always admired Abraham Lincoln for his courage to abolish slavery in the United States.

The next stop was the Washington Monument, a tall tower that was topped by a pyramid-shaped capstone. The bus driver told the band members that the outer walls were made of marble, and the capstone at the top was solid aluminum.

"Let's walk to the top," Jeanne said.

"I have a better idea," Miss Lum said. "Let's take the elevator." The two chaperones agreed with her, laughing.

"Oh, come on," Rose said, getting into the spirit of it. "We can count the stairs."

"And it'll keep us warm," Lizzie added.

What felt like a thousand years later, Rose had nearly reached the top. "Eight hundred and ninety-six..." She had counted the steps the whole way. "Eight hundred and ninety-seven, eight hundred and ninety-eight, eight hundred and—"

"You can stop now, Rose," Lizzie said, gasping for breath. "We're there."

"You made it!" Miss Lum cheered, greeting them with a smile. "How many steps were there? "

Rose took a deep breath. "There were eight hundred and ninety—" Her mind went blank. "Oh, no," she cried. "I forgot!"

Lizzie and Rose both started laughing.

But she forgot about the steps when Miss Lum pointed

out the beautiful view. Sprawled out below, Washington looked like a miniature city made of fancy building blocks. Off to the left Rose could see the White House, and to the right the Capitol. Just beyond that was the U.S. Supreme Court building.

"It's beautiful," Lizzie said. "But I think I'm getting dizzy. I'll meet you downstairs."

By the time the elevator arrived, everyone was ready to go. They all piled in together for the trip down.

On the bus again, the driver said, "At least you're all smiling now. It was so gloomy in here before, I thought it was going to rain on the bus."

Rose smiled. She did feel better after climbing all those stairs—however many there were.

"Our last stop is the Thomas Jefferson Memorial," the bus driver said. "It's on the southern bank of the Tidal Basin. It's beautiful in the spring, but right now it will be cold and windy."

In fact, it was so cold and windy, the jazz band decided to stay on the bus. But Rose admired it through the window. It was a pretty monument, with its rounded dome and all its columns, and it was located right on the edge of the water. Rose hoped she could come back with her family someday, maybe in the spring when all the cherry trees were in bloom.

On the way back to the hotel, Jeanne started everyone singing tunes from *The Sound of Music*. Even Miss Lum and the driver joined in. They swayed back and forth as they sang, and they were just finishing up "Edelweiss" when they pulled up to their hotel.

"Rest up before dinner, girls," Miss Lum said when they all got off the bus. "We'll eat at six and go to bed early. You have a big day tomorrow—in the morning we'll watch the inaugural parade, and tomorrow night we perform."

Rose's heart flip-flopped. On the one hand she was nervous and excited about the big performance, but on the other hand she was angry that Jazz with Pizzazz wouldn't be playing for the president. It was so unfair. She got out her journal and began describing the day's events and her feelings about them. Writing always helped her think things through.

After an early breakfast the next morning, the girls gathered in the hotel's spacious lobby. Rose could feel the excitement in the air. Jazz with Pizzazz was going to watch the parade from the balcony of one of the conference rooms. After that the band

was going to final practice for their performance that
night.

"Hey, isn't that Mr. Horton, or whatever his name is?"
Lizzie whispered suddenly.

Rose nodded. "Mr. Warton," she corrected Lizzie,
making a face. Then, before she could stop herself, she
darted after him and called out his name.

He whirled around, his usual frown on his face. "Yes?"

Rose suddenly didn't know what to say. "I—uh—we're
with the band, Jazz with Pizzazz, and we were just

wondering why you moved us out of the main ball. We were really looking forward to playing for the president," she blurted out.

Mr. Warton kept frowning. "Something came up, girls. As assistant press secretary on the White House staff, I have a great deal to coordinate. I had to move a few groups around. Now if you'll excuse me..."

"We came all this way," Rose called after him, but he didn't even turn around.

Lizzie sighed. "Well, at least you tried."

Rose shook her head. She had tried, but not hard enough. I'm not going to give up, she vowed to herself.

Chapter Six

ROSE TO THE RESCUE

R ose stared at the phone in her hotel room. She couldn't stop thinking about Mr. Warton and the way he had treated the band.

Suddenly an idea came to her. Hey, I know who can help us, she said to herself.

Before she could talk herself out of it, Rose looked up a number in the phone book, picked up the phone, and dialed.

"*Washington Eagle*. How may I direct your call?" asked a voice.

Rose's heart thumped like the drum in the band. "I'd like to speak to Sandy Mills, please."

The line clicked, and the next thing she heard was, "Sandy Mills here."

"Hi. Uh—this is Rose Hopkins. I'm in Jazz with Pizzazz."

"Oh, hello, Rose," Sandy said pleasantly.

Rose took a big breath, then blurted out the whole story. She told the reporter all about Mr. Warton and how Mrs. Pierce had suddenly given them a new schedule.

There was a long pause. "Did Mr. Warton or Mrs. Pierce ever say exactly why the band was bumped?" Sandy asked.

"No," Rose replied. "Not even after Lizzie and I asked him about it this morning." Rose hesitated for a second. "But the first time he saw us, he seemed really surprised that there were no boys in the band," she added quietly.

"What?" Sandy said. Now the reporter seemed really interested in what Rose was telling her.

Rose repeated what she'd just said.

"That's unbelievable," Sandy murmured. "You mentioned that you have a rehearsal this afternoon, right?" she went on. "Why don't I meet you there and we can talk some more?"

"Okay," Rose said. But suddenly she could feel her stomach tighten. What was Miss Lum going to say when she found out why Sandy was coming to their rehearsal? When she hung up a moment later, Rose was feeling even more uncertain. Maybe calling the reporter hadn't been such a good idea after all.

Rose watched nervously as Sandy and her photographer pulled up some chairs and sat down to watch the band's afternoon rehearsal. While the photographer took some pictures, Sandy wrote in her notebook every once in awhile.

After the rehearsal, Rose hurried over to the reporter, hoping that no one would come over to ask what was going on. She glanced around and saw that Miss Lum was busy with the trombone player, going over some parts.

"I'm glad you called," Sandy said, putting a hand on Rose's shoulder. "I'm going to write an article about what's happened to you girls. But first I'm going to call the White House. The president will be sorry that he changed your schedule once he hears that the *Eagle* is printing a story about it."

Rose gulped. Call the president? "But I don't think he even knows about it," Rose tried to protest. This was not at all what she'd had in mind when she'd phoned the newspaper. "It was Mr. Warton—"

"The president is responsible for the people who work for him," Sandy said.

Rose shook her head. This was getting out of hand. "I really don't think—"

"Don't worry about it," Sandy interrupted. "I've got to get back to the office and write up this story. The president definitely has some questions to answer."

Rose bit her lip as she watched the reporter hurry out of the ballroom. Oh no, she thought, everything is getting blown out of proportion.

Feeling sick, Rose picked up her instrument and went up to her room. The article was going to make Rose, the band, and everyone back in the band's hometown look stupid. The schedule change was totally Mr. Warton's fault, but for some reason the reporter was blaming the president.

With a sigh, Rose flopped back onto the floral print bedspread.

Lizzie gave her a worried look. "What's the matter?" she asked. "Are you nervous about tonight?"

Rose shook her head. Then she quickly told Lizzie what she'd done, and what the reporter was about to do.

Lizzie's eyes widened. "Oh, no, Rose," she murmured.

"I don't know what to do," Rose confessed. "I don't want to get the band in trouble."

"Maybe you should tell Miss Lum," Lizzie suggested.

"Tell Miss Lum?" Rose swallowed hard. "I can't do that, Lizzie. She'll think I'm an idiot for calling the newspaper."

"No she won't," Lizzie reassured Rose. "She may not be happy about it, but she'll understand that you were just trying to help."

A few minutes later, Rose found herself knocking on the door of Miss Lum's hotel room. She didn't want to do what she was about to do, but she knew that Lizzie was right. It was the only way to find a solution to the mess that she had created.

"Come on in, Rose," Miss Lum said when she opened the door. She gave her a bright smile. "I'm so delighted that you were able to step in when our other band member got sick. You're a wonderful addition to the band."

"You're not going to think so when you hear what I

did," Rose mumbled. She clasped her hands together and stared down at them while she related the whole story. "I'm so sorry," she finished. "I didn't know the reporter would make such a big deal out of everything."

"Oh, this is awful," Miss Lum murmured. She dropped onto an easy chair.

"I know I made a mistake, Miss Lum," Rose went on. "But I was angry about the way we were treated."

"I was angry, too," Miss Lum said. "But the president didn't have anything to do with what happened."

"I know," Rose agreed miserably. She had to think of a way to stop Sandy from writing that article. Then something came to her. "What if we called Mrs. Pierce and told her what happened?" she said. "Maybe she can explain everything to Sandy."

Miss Lum stood up. "That's a very good idea, Rose. I'll call her right now."

But Rose shook her head. "It was my mistake, Miss Lum. I think I should be the one to call her and explain."

Miss Lum hesitated. "Okay," she said at last. "But why don't you make the call now, from my room. That way I'll be right here if you need any help."

Rose nodded. Miss Lum handed her Mrs. Pierce's number, and Rose took a deep breath to steady her nerves as she picked up the phone. After a lot of being switched from person to person and waiting on hold, Rose finally heard Mrs. Pierce's voice on the line.

"Hello?"

Quickly, before she could lose her nerve, Rose told Mrs. Pierce the whole story.

There was a long silence.

"Well, you've created quite a mess, Rose," Mrs. Pierce said finally. "It won't be easy to undo this, but maybe I can find a way to stop that story from being printed."

Rose blinked back her tears. "Thank you," she choked out.

Mrs. Pierce seemed to sense how upset Rose was. "I'm glad you called," she said in a gentler tone. "I'm sure it wasn't easy to admit your mistake. I'll see what I can do— okay?"

"Okay," Rose mumbled as she hung up the phone.

Miss Lum put an arm around her shoulder. "Good job, Rose," she said. "Let's try not to worry about it, okay? I'm sure Mrs. Pierce will straighten things out."

Rose nodded, but inside she wasn't so sure. Back in her room, she looked out the big picture window at the bustling city. She'd always dreamed of going to Washington and seeing the president. But getting him into trouble had never, ever been a part of that dream.

After a dinner of inaugural
burgers and presidential
sundaes in the hotel
restaurant, it was time for
the band to change into their
gowns.

"So how do I look?" Lizzie asked, twirling in the center
of the room, her peach colored gown shimmering in the
lamplight. Except for the color, it was exactly like Rose's
dress.

"Totally elegant," Rose said. "How about me?"

"Totally stylish," Lizzie said.

Rose glanced at her reflection. When she'd first seen
the mint-green dress in Ellie's attic, all she could think
about was how beautiful it was. But now she barely
noticed the gown. The only thing she saw in the mirror
was the miserable expression on her face. What if Mrs.
Pierce couldn't stop the publication of the article? The
president would be furious at Jazz with Pizzazz. And the
rest of the band will be furious at me, Rose thought.

The members of the band began to congregate in
Rose and Lizzie's room, oohing and ahing as they
admired each other in their dresses, each of a different
color of the rainbow.

"We are definitely going to be the best-looking band

playing tonight, " Jeanne said when everyone had assembled.

"Even if we're not going to be playing at the main ball," someone added.

Rose flushed. For a few brief minutes, she'd actually managed to forget her troubles. But now she knew she had to admit to everyone what she had done.

Rose told the girls then stared at the floor, waiting for everyone to tell her how upset they were about the dumb mistake she'd made.

Instead the room was completely quiet. Then Jeanne spoke up.

"It sounds like you were just trying to help, Rose," she said softly.

"We were all angry," the clarinet player chimed in. "And I'm sure Mrs. Pierce can stop the reporter from writing that article."

Rose blinked in surprise. "You're not angry?"

"Not yet," Jeanne said in a joking tone. "I mean, I wish you hadn't made that call, but I understand why you did it."

"And it's going to turn out okay," Lizzie added. "You'll see."

The others nodded.

Relief washed through Rose. Her problem hadn't been

completely solved yet, but at least her friends were still on her side.

Just then, Miss Lum burst into the room. She was wearing the same gown as the girls, only in black. "Guess what?" she said excitedly. "I just got a call from the president's press secretary. He apologized profusely for the mix-up and the change of schedule. The president himself said that he'll try to get to our performance tonight!"

"Yippeeee!" Jeanne squealed.

Rose and Lizzie danced around in a circle.

"We're going to see the president!" Lizzie chanted, and soon everyone joined in.

Even Miss Lum danced a little jig before she composed herself and quieted down the band. "The press secretary also mentioned that he's informed Sandy Mills of the misunderstanding and of the president's efforts to come see us."

Rose breathed a sigh of relief. At least she didn't have to worry about that anymore. She was glad everything had worked out.

"It's time to go downstairs to the ball and mingle with the guests," Miss Lum announced. "Look for me at eight-thirty. We perform at nine."

Butterflies suddenly swarmed in Rose's stomach. In

less than two hours she would be performing a saxophone solo before a huge audience—that might even include the president!

Chapter

Seven

A BALL AT
THE BALL

R ose felt like a princess entering the
ballroom. Her dress swished
as she walked, and her "diamond"
bracelet sparkled as it caught the
light from the many glittering
crystal chandeliers.

She marveled at the gathering throng of
elegant guests who filled the room with the festive sound
of their excited conversation. Women dressed in beautiful

gowns made from deep, soft velvet and glistening silk seemed to glow with color as they moved about. The men looked so dignified in their crisp white shirts and black tuxedoes.

Waiters slid through the crowds with trays held high. One waiter stopped in front of her and Lizzie.

"Would you like a canapé?" he asked.

Rose looked at the tiny sandwiches. She took one with an olive stuck to the top with a toothpick.

Lizzie took two. "One for each hand," she joked.

Rose spotted a nearby table covered with glasses, and the girls made their way over to it. Rose reached for one of the drinks.

"This is champagne, ladies," said a waiter, who was manning the table. "Perhaps you'd like some of this punch." He handed them each a glass of fruit punch from the other side of the table.

It tasted deliciously bubbly and fruity, and Rose drank the whole glass down.

She and Lizzie spent the next hour wandering through the ball, admiring the fancy clothes and sampling goodies off the many trays of food.

Suddenly Lizzie grabbed her arm. "Hey, isn't that Johnny Flash?"

"Where?" Rose eagerly looked around for the handsome movie star. She'd forgotten that lots of famous people would be at the ball.

Lizzie pointed. "Look—he's with his wife, Angela Wells."

Rose spotted them under the light of a chandelier. "I can't believe it!"

The girls stood rooted to the spot, staring at the Hollywood stars until Johnny glanced at them. He smiled and waved.

Rose and Lizzie nearly melted into the floor. They turned away, giggling and blushing.

"He waved at us!" Rose exclaimed.

"He smiled too!"

They ran to find some other band members to tell their exciting news.

Jeanne found them first. "Come on," she said. "It's almost time for our performance."

A while later the band had gathered near the stage. "Now remember," Miss Lum reminded the girls, "the president said he'd try to make it. There are no guarantees. But let's do our best anyway."

"Just remember Johnny Flash is out there," Lizzie sang out as they climbed the steps up to the stage and got settled.

Rose's mouth felt dry, and her fingers shook as she put them in position on the keys of the saxophone. From up on the stage, she could see how huge the crowd was. What if she made a mistake?

Miss Lum tapped her baton on her music stand to get everyone's attention. She counted silently, then jumped into a Count Basie tune.

As soon as she played her first note, Rose's nervousness drained away. Her lips tightened around the mouthpiece and her fingers flew.

When it was finally time for her solo, Rose stood up. She quickly glanced around, amazed at the number of people who were watching the band perform. And there were the president and first lady! They were just coming into the ballroom, surrounded by friends and Secret Service people.

Rose took a deep breath and put everything she had into her solo. She amazed even herself. When she sat down, loud applause swirled around her. She smiled happily.

Jeanne nudged her. "Go girl!" she whispered.

The band finished up their finale, then stood as a group and took a bow. People were still clapping as they filed off the stage.

Miss Lum hugged them all with tears in her eyes. "You were fabulous," she cried. "Absolutely stupendous!"

"I saw the president," Rose said.

Lizzie jumped up and down. "I did, too. I saw him clap for your solo, Rose."

Miss Lum looked around. "He's left by now, but he did keep his promise."

"Thanks to Rose," Jeanne said. "If she hadn't called the paper, the president never would have known what happened to us. He wouldn't have heard us play."

Rose was embarrassed by the praise after all the trouble that her phone call had caused. "I made a mess by calling Sandy Mills. I shouldn't have opened my big mouth, but I'm glad it all worked out."

Just then someone coughed to get their attention. They turned to see Mr. Warton standing there in a tuxedo. This time he wasn't frowning.

"I just want to tell you ladies that you did a wonderful job tonight," he said. "I'm truly sorry about the mix-up."

"Mix-up?" Rose repeated suspiciously.

Mr. Warton looked apologetic. "When I saw you, I jumped to conclusions," he admitted. "Planning the inauguration balls is an important job. And frankly, I didn't expect nine girls your age to be able to play so well."

"Even after hearing the tape that we sent in?" Lizzie wondered.

Mr. Warton nodded sheepishly. "My attitude seems quite silly now, I must admit. But I want you to know that the President was very impressed with you all. He told me himself as he was leaving." He mumbled good-bye, then disappeared into the crowd.

"I guess we showed him!" Rose exclaimed. Lizzie grinned with delight.

Even Miss Lum looked shocked that Mr. Warton had actually said something nice to them. "Well, he certainly wasn't saying anything about us that we didn't know already! You, young ladies, are wonderful and a superb jazz band. Congratulations."

Then everyone hugged each other. Miss Lum had tears in her eyes again. She was so happy, she gave them permission to stay at the ball for another hour. Half the band went off in search of Johnny Flash, while the other half went to find more food.

"Are you coming?" Lizzie asked Rose.

She nodded. "I'll come find you in a second."

But as Lizzie hurried after the others, Rose made her

way through the crowds to the entrance of the ballroom. She was so glad everything had worked out, and she had actually seen the president of the United States—it was a dream come true.

But now it was time to go home. Rose followed the arrows to the ladies' room. In the sitting area, she looked into the tall mirror that practically covered the entire wall. She curtsied, dipping her head low as if she were meeting royalty. When she looked up again, she was back in Ellie's attic.

FACING THE MUSIC

R ose took one last look at herself in the mirror before she carefully put the saxophone back in the trunk. Next she slipped off the gown and got into her own clothes. Taking one last look around to make sure everything was in place, she turned off the light and raced downstairs.

"I'm still in the kitchen," Ellie called.

Rose put away the key and dashed in to say good-bye to her friend.

"My, my, but you look better," Ellie said with a smile. She clipped the stem off a bushy herb and sniffed it before she tied it with another bunch.

"I feel better, too," Rose said, sniffing the herb Ellie held up to her nose. "Mmmm, oregano."

"That's right," Ellie replied. "It's a special variety that comes all the way from Italy. Would you like to take some home to your grandfather?"

"Sure," Rose said.

"And here's some tarragon and lavender, too. Your mother might like them."

"Thank you," Rose said, carefully holding the herbs.

"And thank you for visiting me," Ellie said with a smile. "Now you'd better hurry home before your mother gets there."

Rose wondered how Ellie always seemed to know everything that was going on. "Good-bye, and thank you again," Rose said before she ran out.

"*Arrivederci!*" Ellie called after her. "Come again."

Outside, the air was a lot colder than it had been

when the sun was out. Rose ran all the way home to keep warm.

Just as she careened up the front walk, her mother pulled into the driveway. Rose retrieved her pink soccer ball from the front step, still carefully holding the herbs in her other hand.

"Hi, Mom."

Her mother looked tired. "Hello, honey. What happened?"

Despite her uneasiness, Rose couldn't help laughing. "You can always tell when something is wrong."

Mrs. Hopkins looked alarmed. "Are you okay? Is someone hurt? Where's Grandfather?"

"It's nothing like that. It's just that I—" Rose shifted the soccer ball in her arms—"I kicked my soccer ball into the street and broke somebody's lamp," she blurted out.

"A lamp?" Her mother raised her eyebrows. "How did you break a lamp?"

Rose pointed across the street. "It was in that car." She followed her mother into the house, carrying her book bag for her.

"I was showing my friends how to kick the soccer ball," Rose continued. "I guess I kicked it too hard."

"I guess so," Mrs. Hopkins said, dropping her books and bags onto the kitchen table and then collapsing into a chair.

"And that's not all," Rose confessed.

Her mother didn't say anything. From the way her mouth turned down at the corners, Rose could tell she wasn't pleased.

"I haven't copied the files for you yet. But I'll do it tonight, and if I don't finish before bedtime, I'll get up early tomorrow morning," Rose rushed on. "I'm really sorry, Mom. It was my responsibility and I let you down."

Mrs. Hopkins took Rose's hand and pulled her forward. Then she stood up and hugged her. "Thank you for telling me the truth. Accidents happen. That car belongs to Mrs. Wentworth's sister, who is visiting from out of state. We'll go over and tell her what happened. As for the files. . ."

"I promise I'll get them done," Rose said, hugging her mother back.

"I know you will," Mrs. Hopkins said with a smile. "And I have a few more to add to the list."

"But—I mean, okay," Rose said. She smiled when her mother started to laugh because Rose had been about to object. She really didn't have anything to complain about, she decided.

"Let's go talk to Mrs. Wentworth's sister," Mrs. Hopkins said.

Rose nodded. "Just a second, though." She ran up to her grandfather's bedroom and knocked.

When he opened the door and smiled at her, she hugged him as tightly as she could. "I love you," she said, then she ran back to her mother. She knew her grandfather would understand that she was feeling better now.

Rose and her mother walked across the street and rang the doorbell. After Rose explained what had happened to Mrs. Richardson, Mrs. Wentworth's sister, she added, "And it was really my fault, even though my friends wrote their names on the note, too."

"Those are certainly good friends you have," Mrs. Richardson said.

"I'll pay for the damage," Rose said, hoping the expense wouldn't make her broke forever.

Mrs. Richardson thought for a moment. "I tell you what—you can pay for half of it. I'm the one who foolishly left a valuable lamp sitting in the car."

Rose's spirits rose until Mrs. Richardson said how much the lamp cost.

"Oh," Rose choked out. "That much?"

Suddenly Mrs. Richardson's eyes twinkled. "Actually, I have another idea," she said. "My sister tells me that…"

Rose listened carefully. When Mrs. Richardson was finished explaining her idea, Rose grinned.

"It's a deal!" she exclaimed.

Diary

Dear Diary,

I still can't believe that everything worked out so well. Mrs. Richardson told me that she'd heard I was a whiz on the computer. Her idea was for me to give her lessons in exchange for my share of the cost of getting the lamp fixed. Boy, did I think that was a good idea. And when I told Ali, Megan, Keisha, and Heather that they didn't have to help me pay for the lamp, they all hugged me. They were happy, too.

I loved seeing the president while I was on my adventure in Washington. But my favorite thing of all was visiting the Lincoln Memorial. That statue of Abraham Lincoln is so cool. I'm going to ask my mom if our family can visit the capital this summer.

It's late and I have to get to bed, but I want to tell you one more thing. Admitting my mistakes to Mrs. Pierce and Miss Lum was really hard. So

was telling my mom that I hadn't finished copying

her files. But once I talked about my mistakes, and

took responsibility for them, I felt a lot better.

And you know what? I bet "Honest Abe" would

be really proud of me!

Love,

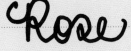

JOIN THE MAGIC ATTIC CLUB!

You can enjoy every adventure of the Magic Attic Club just by reading all the books. And there's more!

You can have a whole world of fun with the dolls, outfits, and accessories that are based on the books. And since Alison, Keisha, Heather, and Megan can wear one another's clothes, you can relive their adventures, or create new ones of your own!

To join the Magic Attic Club, just fill out this postcard and drop it in the mail, or call toll free **1-800-775-9272**. We'll send you a **free** membership kit including a membership card, a poster, stickers, postcards, and a catalog with all four dolls.

With your first purchase of a doll, you'll also receive your own key to the attic. And it's FREE!

Yes, I want to join the Magic Attic Club!

My name is _____

My address is _____

City _____ State _____ Zip _____

Birth date _____ Parent's Signature _____

966

And send a catalog to my friend, too!

My friend's name is _____

Address _____

City _____ State _____ Zip _____

967

If someone has already used the postcard from
this book and you would like a free Magic Attic Club
catalog, just send your full name and address to:

Magic Attic Club
866 Spring Street
P.O. Box 9712
Portland, ME 04104-9954

Or call toll free
1-800-775-9272

Code: 968